Pooh's Quiz Book

E. P. Dutton   New York

POOH's
QUIZ BOOK

❧ by A. A. MILNE ❧

illustrations by E. H. Shepard

Compilation copyright © 1977 by Sir Henry Chisholm, John Frederick Lehmann, John Christopher Medley and Michael John Brown, Trustees of the Pooh Properties

Individual copyrights for text and illustrations: *Winnie-the-Pooh*, Copyright, 1926, by E. P. Dutton & Co., Inc. Copyright Renewal, 1954, by A. A. Milne, *The House at Pooh Corner*, Copyright, 1928, by E. P. Dutton & Co., Inc. Copyright Renewal, 1956, by A. A. Milne

Library of Congress Number: 77-6204
ISBN: 0-525-37485-X

Published in the United States by E. P. Dutton, a Division of Sequoia-Elsevier Publishing Company, Inc., New York

Published simultaneously in Canada by McClelland and Stewart, Ltd.

Editor: Ann Troy   Designer: Riki Levinson

Printed in the U.S.A.   First Edition
10 9 8 7 6 5 4 3 2 1

CIP Data faces the half title page.

Who found the Tail?
  "I," said Pooh,
"At a quarter to two
    (Only it was quarter to eleven really),
  I found the Tail!"

Where does Pooh
find Eeyore's tail?

At Owl's house.

"Handsome bell-rope, isn't it?" said Owl.
Pooh nodded.
"It reminds me of something," he said,
"but I can't think what."

—*Winnie-the-Pooh*

PLEZ CNOKE
IF AN RNSR
IS NOT REQID

Why did Pooh get stuck
in Rabbit's hole?

He ate too much.

"It all comes," said Pooh crossly,
"of not having front doors big enough."

"It all comes," said Rabbit sternly,
"of eating too much. I thought at the time,"
said Rabbit, "only I didn't like to say
anything," said Rabbit, "that one of us
was eating too much," said Rabbit, "and
I knew it wasn't *me*," he said.

—*Winnie-the-Pooh*

Who lives behind a green door
in another part of the forest?

Christopher Robin.

So Winnie-the-Pooh went round to
his friend Christopher Robin, who lived
behind a green door in another part of
the forest.

"Good morning, Christopher Robin."

"Good morning, Winnie-*ther*-Pooh."

—*Winnie-the-Pooh*

Why does Pooh ask Christopher Robin for a balloon?

To get honey.

"What do you want a balloon for?"

Winnie-the-Pooh looked round to see
that nobody was listening, put his paw to
his mouth, and said in a deep whisper:
"*Honey!*"

"But you don't get honey with balloons!"

"*I* do," said Pooh.   —*Winnie-the-Pooh*

Whose house was in the middle
of a beech-tree?

Piglet's.

What was next to his house?

A piece of broken board
which had: "TRESPASSERS W" on it.

Who carries her family
around in her pocket?

Kanga.

"Here—we—are," said Rabbit very slowly and carefully, "all—of—us, and then, suddenly, we wake up one morning and, what do we find? We find a Strange Animal among us. An animal of whom we have never even heard before! An animal who carries her family about with her in her pocket!"

—*Winnie-the-Pooh*

Who jumped into Kanga's pocket
instead of Roo?

Piglet.

At the moment that Kanga's head was turned, Rabbit said in a loud voice, "In you go, Roo!" and in jumped Piglet into Kanga's pocket, and off scampered Rabbit, with Roo in his paws, as fast as he could.

—*Winnie-the-Pooh*

How does Pooh spell honey?

Hunny.

As soon as he got home, he went to the larder; and he stood on a chair, and took down a very large jar of honey from the top shelf. It had HUNNY written on it.

—*Winnie-the-Pooh*

How does Owl spell his name?

WOL.

Owl, wise though he was in many ways,
able to read and write and spell his own
name WOL, somehow went all to pieces
over delicate words. —*Winnie-the-Pooh*

What does Rabbit hang his towels on?

The back of Pooh's legs when he's
stuck in Rabbit's door.

"And I say, old fellow, you're taking up a good deal of room in my house—*do* you mind if I use your back legs as a towel-horse? Because, I mean, there they are—doing nothing—and it would be very convenient just to hang the towels on them."   —*Winnie-the-Pooh*

Who was the house
at Pooh Corner built for?

Eeyore.

"*You* have a house, Piglet," said Pooh, "and I have a house, and they are very good houses. And Christopher Robin has a house, and Owl and Kanga and Rabbit have houses, and even Rabbit's friends-and-relations have houses or somethings, but poor Eeyore has nothing. So what I've been thinking is: Let's build him a house."

"That," said Piglet, "is a Grand Idea."

—*The House at Pooh Corner*

What does Tigger really like to eat?

Extract of Malt.

Tigger leant over the back of Roo's chair, and suddenly he put out his tongue, and took one large golollop. The Extract of Malt had gone.

"Tigger *dear!*" said Kanga.

"He's taken my medicine, he's taken my medicine, he's taken my medicine!" sang Roo happily, thinking it was a tremendous joke.

—*The House at Pooh Corner*

What does Christopher Robin
like to do best?

Nothing.

"How do you do Nothing?" asked Pooh, after he had wondered for a long time.

"Well, it's when people call out at you just as you're going off to do it, 'What are you going to do, Christopher Robin,' and you say, 'Oh, nothing,' and then you go and do it."

"Oh, I see," said Pooh.

—*The House at Pooh Corner*

When Pooh, Piglet, and Rabbit
are playing Poohsticks,
who comes floating down the river?

Eeyore.

"Eeyore!" cried everybody.

Looking very calm, very dignified, with his legs in the air, came Eeyore from beneath the bridge.

"It's Eeyore!" cried Roo, terribly excited.

"Is that so?" said Eeyore, getting caught up by a little eddy, and turning slowly round three times. "I wondered."

—*The House at Pooh Corner*

Where do Pooh and
Piglet find Small?

On Pooh's back.

"Pooh!" he cried. "There's something climbing up your back."

"I thought there was," said Pooh.

"It's Small!" cried Piglet.

"Oh, *that's* who it is, is it?" said Pooh.

"Christopher Robin, I've found Small!" cried Piglet.

"Well done, Piglet," said Christopher Robin. —*The House at Pooh Corner*

What habit does Tigger have?

He bounces.

And the Small and Sorry Rabbit
rushed through the mist at the noise, and it
suddenly turned into Tigger; a Friendly
Tigger, a Grand Tigger, a Large and
Helpful Tigger, a Tigger who bounced,
if he bounced at all, in just the beautiful
way a Tigger ought to bounce.

"Oh, Tigger, I *am* glad to see you,"
cried Rabbit. —*The House at Pooh Corner*

What two friends meet
at the Thoughtful Spot?

Pooh and Piglet.

Halfway between Pooh's house and
Piglet's house was a Thoughtful Spot
where they met sometimes when they
had decided to go and see each other,
and as it was warm and out of the wind
they would sit down there for a little and
wonder what they would do now that they
had seen each other.

—*The House at Pooh Corner*

What accident happened
on a very blusterous day?

The tree with Owl's house
in it blew down.

"Pooh," said Owl severely, "did *you* do that?"

"No," said Pooh humbly. "I don't *think* so."

"I think it was the wind," said Piglet. "I think your house has blown down."

"If it was the wind," said Owl, considering the matter, "then it wasn't Pooh's fault. No blame can be attached to him." —*The House at Pooh Corner*

What does Kanga do when she is feeling motherly?

She counts things.

Now it happened that Kanga had
felt rather motherly that morning, and
Wanting to Count Things—like Roo's
vests, and how many pieces of soap there
were left, and the two clean spots in
Tigger's feeder.

—*The House at Pooh Corner*

Whose tracks were Pooh and Piglet
really following on the Woozle hunt?

Their own.

"Do you see, Piglet? Look at their tracks! Three, as it were, Woozles, and one, as it was, Wizzle. *Another Woozle has joined them!*"

And so it seemed to be. There were the tracks; crossing over each other here, getting muddled up with each other there; but, quite plainly every now and then, the tracks of four sets of paws.

—*Winnie-the-Pooh*

How did Pooh and Piglet hope
to catch a Heffalump?

By digging a Very Deep Pit.

Pooh rubbed his nose with his paw, and said that the Heffalump might be walking along, humming a little song, looking up at the sky, and so he wouldn't see the Very Deep Pit until he was halfway down, when it would be too late.

—*Winnie-the-Pooh*

Who discovered the North Pole?

Pooh.

"Pooh," said Christopher Robin, "where did you find that pole?"

Pooh looked at the pole in his hands.

"I just found it," he said. "I thought it ought to be useful. I just picked it up."

"Pooh," said Christopher Robin solemnly, "the Expedition is over. You have found the North Pole!"

"Oh!" said Pooh.   —*Winnie-the-Pooh*

Who rescued Piglet in a boat
made from an umbrella?

Christopher Robin and Pooh.

Christopher Robin opened his umbrella
and put it point downwards in the water.
It floated but wobbled. Then they both got
in it together, and it wobbled no longer.

"I shall call this boat *The Brain of Pooh*,"
said Christopher Robin, and *The Brain of
Pooh* set sail forthwith in a south-westerly
direction, revolving gracefully.

—*Winnie-the-Pooh*

Who picked a bunch
of violets for Eeyore?

Piglet.

Piglet had got up early that morning
to pick himself a bunch of violets; and
when he had picked them and put them
in a pot in the middle of his house, it
suddenly came over him that nobody had
ever picked Eeyore a bunch of violets.

—*The House at Pooh Corner*

What special present did
Christopher Robin give to Pooh?

A pencil case.

When Pooh saw what it was, he nearly fell down, he was so pleased. It was a Special Pencil Case. There were pencils in it marked "B" for Bear, and pencils marked "HB" for Helping Bear, and pencils marked "BB" for Brave Bear.

And they were all for Pooh.

—Winnie-the-Pooh

How old will Pooh be
when Christopher Robin is 100?

99.

"Pooh, *promise* you won't forget about me, ever. Not even when I'm a hundred," said Christopher Robin.

Pooh thought for a little.

"How old shall *I* be then?"

"Ninety-nine."

Pooh nodded.

"I promise," he said.

—*The House at Pooh Corner*